P9-CDP-053

STARK
ENTER THE DRAGON
WRITER - FRED VAN LENTE
PENCILER - JAMES CORDEIRO
INKER - SCOTT KOBLISH
COLORIST - STUDIO F'S MARTEGOD GRACIA
LETTERER - BLAMBOT'S NATE PIEKOS
COVER - MICHAEL GOLDEN
PRODUCTION - IRENE LEE
ASSISTANT EDITOR - NATHAN COSBY
EDITOR - MARK PANICCIA
EDITOR IN CHIEF - JOE QUESADA
PUBLISHER - DAN BUCKLEY
Spotlight
MARVEL®

VISIT US AT
www.abdopublishing.com

Reinforced library bound edition published in 2009 by Spotlight, a division of the ABDO Publishing Group, 8000 West 78th Street, Edina, Minnesota 55439. Spotlight produces high-quality reinforced library bound editions for schools and libraries. Published by agreement with Marvel Characters, Inc.

Library of Congress Cataloging-in-Publication Data

Van Lente, Fred.
Enter the dragon / Fred Van Lente, writer ; James Cordeiro, penciler ; Scott Koblish, inker ; Martegod Gracia, colorist ; Nate Piekos, letterer. -- Reinforced library bound ed.
p. cm. -- (Iron Man)
"Marvel."
ISBN 978-1-59961-552-3
1. Graphic novels. [1. Graphic novels.] I. Cordeiro, James, ill. II. Title.
PZ7.7.V26Ent 2008
[E]--dc22

2008000105

All Spotlight books have reinforced library bindings and are manufactured in the United States of America.

THE REPORTS WE RECEIVED APPEAR TO BE ACCURATE, RHODEY...
...OUR STARK CHINA FACILITY, THREE THOUSAND WORKERS STRONG, LOOKS COMPLETELY DESERTED!
EVERYONE'S JUST...VANISHED!

AREA SCAN: INFRARED
STARK INTERNATIONAL
UH-OH...EVEN THE MACHINERY IS COLD, WHICH MEANS IT HAD TO HAVE BEEN SHUT DOWN DAYS, IF NOT WEEKS AGO.
NOT GOOD.
STARK INTERNATIONAL CORPORATE HEADQUARTERS IN LONG ISLAND:
IT TOOK FOUR WHOLE DAYS FOR THE LETTERS FROM THE WORKERS' FREAKED-OUT FAMILIES TO MAKE THEIR WAY UP THE COMPANY FOOD CHAIN TO US IN THE FIRST PLACE, TONE.
WHICH REMINDS ME...DID YOU HAVE ANY TIME TO THINK ABOUT WHAT I SAI--?
LOOK ALIVE, JIMBO!
WITH THE BIG BOSS OFF IN CHINA YOU'RE MY TONY-AWAY-FROM-TONY!
I GOT FIFTEEN LETTERS, EIGHT CHECKS, THREE PERSONNEL TRANSFERS AND ONE GET-WELL CARD THAT NEEDS YOUR HANCOCK, MR. CHIEF OPERATING OFFICER!
GEEZ, GIRL!
DON'T YOU KNOCK?
SORRY...I DIDN'T REALIZE YOU WERE SO...HARD AT WORK IN HERE.
TELL ME ABOUT IT! IF I HAD KNOWN THE PRIVATE SECTOR WAS THIS STRESSFUL, I NEVER WOULDA LEFT THE SERVICE!

PHEW! SHE'S GONE, TONY!
BUT SHE KINDA MADE MY POINT FOR ME, THERE.
WHICH WAS... WHAT, AGAIN?
EVERYONE AT H.Q. KNOWS IT WAS TONY STARK WHO LEFT FOR CHINA...
... BUT IT'S IRON MAN WHO SHOWS UP THERE!
I KNOW SHELLHEAD'S COVER IS THAT YOU MADE HIM HEAD OF SECURITY, BUT IF HE KEEPS SHOWING UP WHERE YOU'RE SUPPOSED TO BE, DON'T YOU THINK PEOPLE ARE GONNA PUT TWO AND TWO TOGETHER?
I HEAR YOU, BUT I CAN'T THINK ABOUT "SECRET IDENTITIES" WHEN MY EMPLOYEES ARE IN DANGER, RHODEY.
S.I. SET UP THIS PLANT ON THE MONGOLIAN BORDER IN AN ECONOMIC PARTNERSHIP WITH THE CHINESE GOVERNMENT BECAUSE THE PROVINCE IS SO ISOLATED.
THE ARMOR WAS THE QUICKEST WAY OUT HERE...
...HMMM...
...SOME KIND OF WEIRD ENERGY TRAIL HEADING OFF TOWARD THOSE MOUNTAINS IN THE DISTANCE.
AREA SCAN: EXPAND SPECTRAL DENSITY
SINCE THERE'S NO SIGN OF A STRUGGLE OR ANY OTHER CLUES AT THE PLANT ITSELF...
...IT'S THE ONLY LEAD WORTH FOLLOWING!

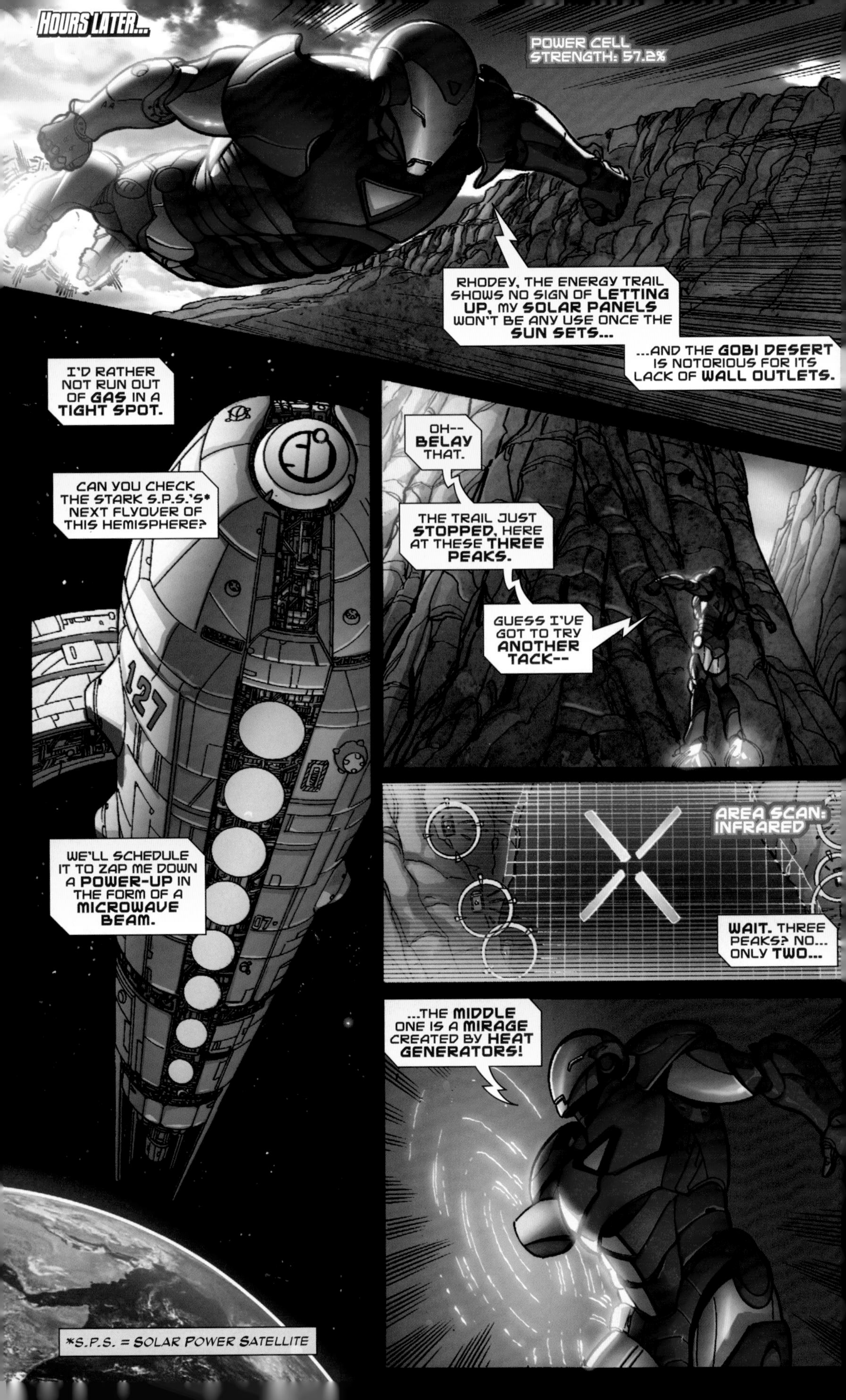
HOURS LATER...
POWER CELL STRENGTH: 57.2%
RHODEY, THE ENERGY TRAIL SHOWS NO SIGN OF LETTING UP, MY SOLAR PANELS WON'T BE ANY USE ONCE THE SUN SETS...
...AND THE GOBI DESERT IS NOTORIOUS FOR ITS LACK OF WALL OUTLETS.
I'D RATHER NOT RUN OUT OF GAS IN A TIGHT SPOT.
CAN YOU CHECK THE STARK S.P.S.'S* NEXT FLYOVER OF THIS HEMISPHERE?
127
WE'LL SCHEDULE IT TO ZAP ME DOWN A POWER-UP IN THE FORM OF A MICROWAVE BEAM.
*S.P.S. = SOLAR POWER SATELLITE
OH-- BELAY THAT.
THE TRAIL JUST STOPPED, HERE AT THESE THREE PEAKS.
GUESS I'VE GOT TO TRY ANOTHER TACK--
AREA SCAN: INFRARED
WAIT. THREE PEAKS? NO... ONLY TWO...
...THE MIDDLE ONE IS A MIRAGE CREATED BY HEAT GENERATORS!

WELL.
HERE'S SOMETHING YOU DON'T SEE EVERY DAY.
EXTERIOR COATING: SHIFT TO: CAMOUFLAGE MATCH
你好
你好
TRANSLATION FILTER: CHINESE: LOCAL DIALECT: JIN (INNER MONGOLIA)
⟨HEY. HEY, BUDDY.⟩
⟨YEAH?⟩
⟨HELP A GUY OUT, WILLYA-- WHO'S IN CHARGE HERE?⟩
⟨YOU MEAN YOU DON'T KNOW? WHERE HAVE YOU BEEN?⟩
⟨OUT SICK! AREN'T WE SUPPOSED TO BE WORKING FOR STARK?⟩
⟨SHHH! DON'T SAY THAT NAME SO LOUD! YOU WANNA GET PUNCHED IN THE MOUTH?⟩
⟨THE MANDARIN HAS SAVED US FROM SLAVERY TO THAT FOREIGN DOG!⟩

<HE'S THE DESCENDANT OF HISTORY'S GREATEST CONQUEROR, GENGHIS KHAN-- ALL OF CHINA IS HIS BY BIRTHRIGHT!>
<ONCE WE HELP HIM FINISH BUILDING HIS SECRET WEAPON, HE'LL VANQUISH THE GOVERNMENT! OUR PROVINCE WILL REAP THE REWARDS OF LOYALTY TO HIM--WITHOUT BEING BOUND TO TONY STARK! PTUI!>
<BUT HOW COME YOU DON'T ALREADY KNOW THA--?>
<HELLO?>
MIND CONTROL
ICE
LIGHTNING
FIRE
LIGHT
CONCUSSION
VORTEX
DARKNESS
MATTER REARRANGER
YOU GETTING ALL THIS, RHODEY?
YEAH, THE MANDARIN--HE'S THE DUDE WITH THE BLING THAT STINGS!
THOSE KOOKY RINGS OF HIS GOT MORE GADGETS IN THEM THAN A SWISS ARMY KNIFE ON STEROIDS!
NO, I MEAN...ABOUT THE WORKERS HATING ME. I--I THOUGHT WE WERE HELPING THEM...
I KNOW, MAN, THAT'S TOUGH TO HEAR. NOBODY'S SAYING YOUR BILLIONS AND BILLIONS OF DOLLARS MAKE YOU UNABLE TO RELATE TO THE AVERAGE JOE, BUT...
...UH...

BUT?
JUST A SECOND, I GOTTA THINK OF A WAY TO FINISH THAT SENTENCE...
HOLD ON--
SENSORS ARE DETECTING A SUDDEN SPIKE OF THAT WEIRD ENERGY THAT LED ME HERE--
AH! STARK'S ARMORED LAP-DOG. WELCOME! YOUR APPEARANCE HERE IS MOST PREDICTABLE!
KRAKABOOM
IN FACT, I HAVE BEEN TRACKING YOUR PROGRESS SINCE YOU LEFT YOUR MASTER'S PLANT!
SHKRAM
CAN'T SAY I COULD'VE GUESSED YOU'D STOOP TO MASS KIDNAPPING, MANDARIN.
THAT SEEMS PETTY EVEN BY YOUR STANDARDS.
"KIDNAPPING?!"

THE MONGOL TRIBES FOLLOWED THE GREAT KHAN BECAUSE HE PROMISED--THEN DELIVERED--GLORY!
AS HIS RIGHTFUL HEIR, THE PEOPLE FOLLOW ME FOR THE SAME REASON-- OF THEIR OWN FREE WILL!
I DO NOT EXPECT A FOREIGNER TO UNDERSTAND!
YOUR HELMET CAN ADJUST TO MY LIGHTNESS RING--OR MY DARKNESS RING--
EYESLITS: DARKEN AGAINST: HIGH-INTENSITY LIGHT
EYESLITS: LIGHTEN AGAINST: HIGH-INTENSITY DARKNESS--
--BUT CAN THEY ADJUST TO BOTH AT ONCE, I WONDER?
EYESLITS: ERROR%: ERROR%: ERROR%
Ah. I THOUGHT NOT.
WHAM
KRASH
CAUTIO
TONE? TONE!?
Aw, NO--HE'S OUT COLD!

QUICKLY, SLAVES!
STRIP THE INTRUDER OF HIS ARMOR.
USER: UNRESPONSIVE
PERHAPS WE COULD USE IT FOR SCRAP.
AUTO-DEFENSE MODE: ACTIVATED
SHIFTING TO: INTERNAL OXYGEN SUPPLY
SHUMP
SHUMP
STEP AWAY FROM THE ARMOR.
THIS ARMOR IS PROTECTED BY STARK-TRONICS VEHICLE SECURITY.
STEP AWAY FROM THE ARMOR AND YOU WILL NOT BE HARMED.
STOP STALLING, YOU GUTLESS FOOLS!
THAT ARMOR IS MINE AS SPOILS OF WAR!

NON-LETHAL DETERRENT: ACTIVATED
SONAR: ACTIVATED
TAKING: EVASIVE ACTION
AUTOPILOT: TARGET COORDINATES: PUBLIC AREA: 100 KM SOUTHEAST
<FASCINATING.>
<SHALL WE GIVE PURSUIT, O GREAT KHAN?>
<NO. IT IS TOO LATE FOR IRON MAN, OR TONY STARK, OR ANYONE ELSE TO STOP ME.>

⟨SOUND THE ORDER! EVERYONE! ALL ABOARD!⟩
⟨WHEN THE GLORIOUS HISTORY OF MY NEW KHANATE IS WRITTEN, GENERATIONS HENCE...⟩
⟨...THIS DAY SHALL BE KNOWN...⟩
⟨...AS THE DAWN OF THE MANDARIN DYNASTY!⟩
VVRRRRRMMMMM

PURSUIT? NEGATIVE
LOCAL HOSTILES? NEGATIVE
COMMENCE: USER REVIVAL

ADMINISTER: SMELLING SALTS
FSSSS
shump
shump
WUNNH!

I DON'T BELIEVE IT! I LIVE IN LONG ISLAND BUT I GOTTA COME ALL THE WAY TO THE GREAT WALL O' CHINA TO MEET IRON MAN
MAURIE, TAKE OUR PICTURE!
WHERE...?

WELCOME BACK TO CONSCIOUSNESS, TONE.
AS PER PRE-PROGRAMMED PROTOCOLS, ARMOR AUTOPILOT FLEW YOU TO THE NEAREST PUBLIC AREA.
WELL...I NEED YOU TO PLOT THE COORDINATES TO MANDARIN'S BASE FOR A RETURN FLIGHT.
EVEN IF MY WORKERS HAVE TURNED AGAINST ME, I CAN'T JUST LEAVE THEM IN HIS CLUTCHES--

RRUMBLY
WHOA! WHAT WAS THAT?
WAS IT GOOD OR BAD?

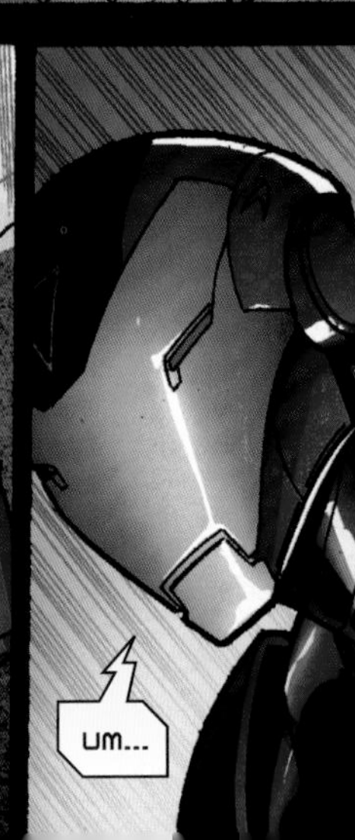
UM...

...I'M GOING TO HAVE TO GO WITH "BAD."
BOOM

BEIJING. THE GREAT HALL OF THE PEOPLE.
ROAARRR
<MEMBERS OF THE CENTRAL COMMITTEE! YOUR OPTIONS ARE SIMPLE:>
<RECOGNIZE MY SOVEREIGNTY...OR BE DESTROYED!>
<MY RULE CLEARLY HAS THE MANDATE OF HEAVEN!>
<I HAVE CHINA'S VERY MYTHS AND LEGENDS AT MY BECK AND CALL!>
<NOW KNEEL BEFORE YOUR RIGHTFUL KHAN!>

MANDY COULD GIVE EVEN YOU A RUN FOR YOUR MONEY IN THE INVENTOR OLYMPICS, TONE.
PUFF THE MAGIC DRAGON IS MADE OUTTA THAT NEW HIGH-STRENGTH ALUMINUM-YTTRIUM-NICKEL ALLOY... INTERNAL ANTI-GRAV UNITS KEEP IT IN THE AIR... ITS SCALES ARE A SERIES OF ADVANCED SOLAR ARRAYS...
I FEEL LIKE A BUMBLEBEE TRYING TO TAKE DOWN A JETLINER.
THE S.I. MAINFRAME MAKE ANY SENSE OF THE ARMOR'S SPECTRO-ANALYSIS OF THIS THING?
SOLAR ARRAYS? OKAY--LISTEN CAREFULLY-- OUR S.P.S. SHOULD BE PASSING OVER BEIJING RIGHT ABOUT NOW, RIGHT?
I NEED YOU TO POWER IT UP IMMEDIATELY AND BEAM ME DOWN EVERY JOULE OF SUNLIGHT IT'S GOT STORED!
EVERY...? Uh, TONY, I'M NOT SURE THAT'S SUCH A GREAT--
TRUST ME!
NOW I'VE JUST GOT TO GET MANDARIN'S ATTENTION...
...WHICH COULD BE A CHALLENGE IN ITSELF...
<Aaahh... MY THANKS, IRON MAN, FOR SPARING ME THE EFFORT OF TRACKING YOU DOWN.>

ROOAR
RHODEY...
HEY! THIS IS YOUR CRAZY PLAN, REMEMBER?
IT'S GONNA TAKE AT LEAST SIXTY SECONDS FOR THE SATELLITE TO POWER UP ALL THE WAY!
YOU GOTTA STALL THAT THING--
JAMES RHODES!
AAAAH!
WHAT? WHAT?
CAN I TALK TO YOU?
Um, ACTUALLY, I'M KIND OF IN THE MIDDLE OF--
YOU KNOW, I BUST MY TAIL EVERY DAY TO KEEP THIS COMPANY RUNNING SMOOTHLY!
DID I EVER SAY YOU DIDN--
AND MY JOB IS EXTRA HARD WHEN TONY IS AWAY!
THAT'S WHY I'M BEHIND YOU ONE HUNDRED AND TEN PERC--
SO I CAN'T HELP BUT GET A LITTLE PERTURBED THAT EVERY TIME I WALK PAST HERE YOU'RE PLAYING COMPUTER SOLITAIRE AND TALKING ON THE PHONE WITH YOUR FRIENDS!
B-BUT--

RHO... RHODE...
WARNING! SURFACE PRESSURE EXCEEDING STRESS LIMITS! WARNING!
I DON'T BELIEVE THIS! YOU'RE NOT EVEN LOOKING AT ME WHILE I'M TALKING TO YOU!
WELL, Uh, Y'SEE, PEPPER...
...THE TRUTH IS...
COMPLETE
CHOMP
...I'M TOTALLY ADDICTED TO SOLITAIRE!
HEY, LOOK, THERE'S THE KING I NEEDED!
CLICK
COMPLETE

AAAAAGGHHH!
‹POWER SURGE--CAN'T CONTROL--›

KRASH

THANKS, PEPPER, FOR HELPING ME REALIZE I HAVE A PROBLEM, WHICH IS THE FIRST STEP TOWARD SOLVING IT--
WHATEVER! YOU AND TONY ARE TWO PEAS IN A POD...
MAN-CHILDREN!
YOU MAY HAVE SAVED BEIJING, BUT YOU'VE SEALED YOUR DOOM, IRON MAN!
I CAN STILL OVERWHELM YOU WITH SHEER NUMBERS!
UNUSUAL ENERGY: SOURCE LOCATED
YOU DON'T SAY...
HORDES OF YOUR MASTER'S WORKERS-- UNARMED BUT FOR THEIR HATRED FOR YOU AND STARK!
THEY'LL JUST KEEP COMING AT YOU, OVER AND OVER, WAVE AFTER WAVE, IN SERVICE TO THEIR KHAN, UNTIL YOU AT LAST FALL!
ENERGY SOURCE DETERMINED TO BE:
RING: RIGHT RING FINGER

UNI-BEAM COHERENCY: NARROWEST SETTING
SPAK
WHAT...?
<MY MIND--MY THOUGHTS--THEY'RE MINE AGAIN!>
<WE'VE BEEN RELEASED FROM THE MANDARIN'S CONTROL SOMEHOW!>
<STOP! STOP, MY SUBJECTS! IT IS BLASPHEMY TO DEFY YOUR KHAN!>
<GRAB HIM--TAKE HIS RINGS--MAKE SURE HE CAN'T HURT ANY MORE PEOPLE!>
<WHAT A CROCK! I CAN'T BELIEVE HE MADE US SPOUT THAT "KHAN" NONSENSE!>
PLEASE CONVEY OUR APOLOGIES TO MR. STARK, IRON MAN.
WE HAD NO WISH TO LEAVE OUR POSTS AT HIS FACTORY, BUT OUR WILLS WERE ENSLAVED BY THE MANDARIN'S MIND-CONTROL RING.
UNDER THE CIRCUMSTANCES, I'M SURE MR. STARK WILL MORE THAN UNDERSTAND.

LATER THAT WEEK...
...SO, AGAIN, I'D LIKE TO THANK IRON MAN FOR JOINING US SO SOON AFTER THE CEREMONY HONORING HIM FOR SAVING BEIJING!
HIS PRESENCE HERE IS ONLY FITTING FOR THIS GRAND RE-DEDICATION OF THE STARK CHINA FACILITY!
<A TOAST! TO MR. STARK!>
<TO MR. STARK!>
PLEASE! I'M JUST HAPPY YOU'RE ALL SAFE AND SURVIVED YOUR ORDEAL.
IT'S ME WHO'S TOASTING YOU.
EAT, DRINK, AND BE MERRY! I'LL REJOIN YOU SHORTLY...
...AFTER I'VE HAD A WORD WITH MY BODY-GUARD.

I HAVE NO IDEA HOW YOU CAN WEAR THIS SARDINE CAN ALL DAY.
IT'S AN ACQUIRED TASTE, I'LL ADMIT.
UGH! IT REEKS OF SWEAT IN THERE!
I APPRECIATE YOU PUTTING IT ON, HOW-EVER BRIEFLY. THAT SHOULD ALLAY ANY SUSPICIONS THAT TONY STARK AND IRON MAN ARE THE SAME GUY, NO?
BEFORE I FORGET--STARK INTERNATIONAL HUMAN RESOURCES PROTOCOL DICTATES THAT I, AS YOUR IMMEDIATE SUPERVISOR, PERSONALLY HAND YOU A COPY OF THIS.
Huh? WHAT'S--?
YOU'RE PUTTING A REPRIMAND IN MY EMPLOYEE FILE?
WHY ARE YOU PUTTING A REPRIMAND IN MY EMPLOYEE FILE?
ACCORDING TO... UNNAMED SOURCES, YOU SPENT THE ENTIRE TIME I'VE BEEN HERE IN CHINA GOSSIPING LIKE A SCHOOL-GIRL ON THE PHONE...
...THAT IS, WHEN YOU WEREN'T PLAYING VIDEO GAMES.
"VIDEO--?" YOU KNOW I SPENT THAT WHOLE TIME SAVIN' YOUR BACON, TONE!
THIS IS ALL PEPPER'S DOING!
THAT MAY BE, BUT I, OF COURSE, CAN'T CLAIM TO HAVE ANY KNOWLEDGE OTHERWISE...
...WITHOUT JEOPARDIZING THAT PRECIOUS SECRET IDENTITY YOU'RE SO KEEN ON PROTECTING...
KNEW I NEVER SHOULDA LEFT THE SERVICE...
THE END